Moans and Groans and Dinosaur Bones

By Judy Delton
Illustrated by Alan Tiegreen

A Stepping Stone Book™
RANDOM HOUSE 🏠 NEW YORK

For Antigone Karvounarakis Delton:
Hallelujah, we all sing!
(Though someone is off-key.)
Welcome, welcome, Christmas Love,
Our own Antigone!
—J.D.

Text copyright © 1997 by Judy Delton
Illustrations copyright © 1997 by Alan Tiegreen
Cover illustration copyright © 2008 by David Harrington

Originally published by Yearling, an imprint of Random House Children's Books, a division of Random House, Inc., in 1997.

Random House and colophon are registered trademarks and A Stepping Stone Book and colophon are trademarks of Random House, Inc.

Visit us on the Web!
www.steppingstonesbooks.com
www.randomhouse.com/kids

Educators and librarians, for a variety of teaching tools, visit us at
www.randomhouse.com/teachers

Library of Congress Cataloging-in-Publication Data:
Delton, Judy.
Moans and groans and dinosaur bones / by Judy Delton ;
illustrated by Alan Tiegreen.
  p. cm. — (Pee Wee Scouts)
"A Stepping Stone book."
ISBN 978-0-440-40982-3
I. Tiegreen, Alan, ill. II. Title.
PZ7.D388Mj 2008   [Fic]—dc22   2007049647

Printed in the United States of America   14 13 12 11 10 9 8 7 6 5

Contents

Bad Deed
Plans

"**W**inter is boring," sighed Molly Duff to her best friend, Mary Beth Kelly.

"It's too long," said Mary Beth. "And too cold. The snow is all dirty, and my boots leak." She kicked a pile of gray snow.

"Nothing exciting ever happens. Just school and more school and Pee Wee Scout meetings every Tuesday," said Molly.

"Even Pee Wee Scouts is boring in the winter," agreed Mary Beth. The girls were on their way to a Pee Wee Scout meeting.

"I bet we'll just do some project, and Sonny will wreck his with too much glue, and Roger will stick Rachel's braids together. It's so boring," said Molly.

"Let's not go to Pee Wee Scouts!" said Mary Beth. "Let's do something exciting instead!"

Molly stopped in her tracks. Not go to Pee Wee Scouts? What a scary idea! Molly got shivers down her back just thinking about it. Was such a daring thing possible? And what would her mother say when she found out? Unless, of course, she never found out . . .

"What would we do instead?" asked Molly.

"Something," said Mary Beth. "Anything.

Something different than looking at creepy Roger."

"What if we get caught?" said Molly. "It's like playing hooky from school. We could get arrested."

"Pooh," said Mary Beth, waving the idea away with her mitten. "Scouts isn't like school. I mean, there's no law that says you have to go to a Pee Wee Scout meeting. It's something you volunteer to do, like joining the army."

Molly thought about that. Was her friend right? If there was no danger, then why did it feel so scary?

The girls sat down on a park bench to think about it.

"We're going to be late for the meeting," Molly said nervously.

"We're not going to the meeting," said Mary Beth. "While they're having their boring old meeting and talking about good deeds, we're going to be having the time of our lives!"

"Yeah!" shouted Molly. "Good for us!"

The girls sat in silence. Then Molly asked softly, "What are we going to be doing?"

"Well," said her friend, "we could go to a movie."

"I don't have any money," said Molly.

"Or," Mary Beth went on, "we could go sliding on the hill."

Molly looked at the rivers of melting snow running down the street.

"Too wet," she said. "Half the hill is dead grass."

Then Mary Beth jumped up and said, "Let's do something bad instead of something good! Let's do bad deeds instead of good deeds! Let's ring someone's doorbell and run and hide!"

Molly looked at Mary Beth in surprise.

Molly might agree to miss Scouts, but she hadn't lost her senses.

"That's dumb," she said. "I don't feel like being a criminal just because we want to have some fun." Missing a meeting was one thing. Facing her mother across a desk at the police station was definitely something else.

The girls listed things to do. Molly even wrote them on a corner of her spelling test paper. *Make cookies.* No good, because they'd need a stove and then their mothers would know they were skipping Scouts. *Roller-skate.* Too wet. And skates didn't fit over snow boots. *Go to the zoo or the mall.* How would they get there? They didn't drive.

"There isn't much excitement around here," said Mary Beth with a groan. "If we lived in California like Ashley, we could go to Hollywood and see the stars."

"If we lived someplace with a race-track, we could go to a car race. I saw it on TV."

"I guess we live in a boring place," said Mary Beth.

The girls picked up their mittens and their books. They both knew where they were going. Even if they were late and it was boring, Pee Wee Scouts was still the only thing around.

CHAPTER

Good News and Bad News

"**W**here were you guys?" shouted Roger White as the girls walked down Mrs. Peters's basement steps. Mrs. Peters was their troop leader. Troop 23 met in her basement. Sonny's mother, Mrs. Stone, was assistant leader. She was already passing out cupcakes. The same boring kind of cupcakes they had every week, Molly noticed.

"Where were you? Where were you?"

Roger pestered the girls again.

"Nowhere," said Mary Beth.

"Hey, how could you be nowhere?" shouted Tim Noon. "You have to be somewhere!"

"It's good you got here, girls," said Mrs. Peters. "I was just about to tell everyone the big news."

I'll bet, thought Molly. Big news to Mrs. Peters meant things like a visit to a farm to see baby pigs, or a trip to the market to shop for an easy meal as a surprise for their parents. Molly began to wish she'd decided to ring doorbells after all.

"The news," said their leader, "is that we are taking an overnight trip! We are going to Center City on a train, and we'll stay overnight in a hotel! We'll go to the Science and History Museum, where we'll see real dinosaur bones and learn about people who lived in the past."

Molly almost choked on her cupcake. Mary Beth looked stunned.

"We almost missed this meeting because of your silly idea!" she whispered to Molly.

"It was your idea!" said Molly. "Not mine."

But Molly couldn't even remember whose idea it had been. And it didn't matter. Because all of a sudden Pee Wee Scouts appeared to be more exciting than it ever had been in the past. A trip on a real train! Overnight in a real hotel! Dinosaur bones! What a close call that was. She might have missed it all just to go to a movie or to go sliding on brown grass.

Everyone was talking at once.

"Do our parents have to come?" shouted Sonny Stone, glaring at his mother.

"Can we sleep on those little shelf beds on the train?" asked Patty Baker. "And put our clothes in those little net hammocks? I saw that in an old movie."

"I'm scared of trains," said Tim Noon. "Sometimes they crash."

"Scaredy-cat," scoffed Roger White.

"I'm going to sit in the cockpit and help the driver drive."

"He doesn't sit in a cockpit," said Kevin Moe, who knew a lot of things. He was very smart, and Molly wanted to marry him someday. Him or Jody, that is. Jody George was smart too and had a wheelchair he let the Pee Wees ride in sometimes.

"A cockpit is for a pilot in a plane," Kevin went on. "An engineer drives a train."

"My uncle is an engineer," said Kenny Baker. "And he doesn't drive a train, he works in an office."

"That's another kind of engineer," said Jody.

"My uncle's a pilot," said Lisa Ronning. "He flies those jumbo jets across the ocean."

Now everyone wanted to hear about jumbo jets.

Mrs. Peters held up her hands, which meant silence. One by one people stopped talking.

"Remember to raise your hand when you want to speak," she reminded them. "We won't be sleeping on the train, and parents won't be coming, and the train will not crash," she went on.

Rachel Meyers's hand was waving. "Mrs. Peters, I've been to Center City with my aunt and we ate in a fancy restaurant at the top of a big tower and it turned around while we ate. The whole restaurant. Will we be going there?"

"How could a restaurant turn around?" asked Tracy Barnes.

"Maybe it's on wheels or something," said Kenny.

"I don't know if our restaurant will revolve," said Mrs. Peters firmly. "But we'll have a good time. Now I have to tell you the next part of the news. On this trip, we'll earn a brand-new badge."

Before she could say more, the Pee Wees broke into loud cheers. They loved new badges. They had quite a few badges already. One for baby-tending, one for working with pets, and several for helping out in the community. But they could never have too many. A new badge was an exciting thing to hear about.

"What do we have to do on the trip to get a badge?" asked Tracy.

"What's the name of the badge?" asked Patty.

"It will be called our museum badge!" said Mrs. Peters. "Doesn't that sound like fun?"

Mrs. Peters tried to make her voice

sound exciting, but it didn't work. No one looked as if they thought a museum badge was fun. The Pee Wees all groaned.

Their leader made another try. "Just think of all the old things you will see!" she said. "Mummies and dinosaurs and old pots and gold coins. All you have to do to earn your badge is choose your favorite and write a little paper about it or draw a picture of it."

Many of the Pee Wees did not think it was fun to do something they did in school. And writing sounded like school. Molly secretly liked to write. Especially lists and book reports. But she didn't want the other Pee Wees to know that, so she groaned too. But she was already thinking of how hard it might be to choose just *one* thing out of all the things in the museum to write about. She had the feeling she would want to write about quite a few of them. She knew that it was a big museum. She didn't want to draw a picture. That was for babies. It was for the Pee Wees who were too lazy to write, like Roger, thought Molly. Roger would probably draw a picture. When the Pee Wees had been working on a badge for reading, Roger took baby books out of the library instead of real books. It was like cheating.

"Mrs. Peters, can we write a paper *and* draw a picture?" asked Rachel.

Rachel was a show-off sometimes, thought Molly. Even if Molly wanted to do both, she wouldn't brag about it.

"I suppose so," said Mrs. Peters to Rachel.

"I guess a picture or a paper won't be so bad," said Mary Beth.

"Now for the last thing," said their leader. "I need one more parent to help me on the trip, since Mrs. Stone can't leave the twins alone and Mr. Stone is out of town." Larry Stone was Sonny's adoptive dad. Sonny looked relieved.

The other Pee Wees looked worried. No one wanted their parents there.

"She said parents weren't coming," grumbled Lisa.

"It would spoil the trip for whoever had their parents along," whispered Mary Beth. "I sure hope mine don't volunteer."

Rachel's hand was waving again. "My mom or dad can come," she said.

"Why would Rachel *want* her parents there?" Tracy said to Molly.

Molly didn't know. She was just glad her own mother worked on weekends.

"My parents could come, too," said Jody.

Jody was so good-hearted, he wouldn't even mind having his parents around, thought Molly.

"You didn't let me finish. I already have a parent who has volunteered to come," said Mrs. Peters. "I am pleased to say that Molly's mother, Mrs. Duff, has agreed to take some time off work to help out."

Double Trouble

Molly couldn't believe her ears! In one minute, one second even, her trip had been ruined. The other Pee Wees made comforting noises. They could afford to feel bad for her, she thought. They were safe. They knew their own parents would be at home, where they belonged. Even though Jody and Rachel might not mind, the rest of the Pee Wees definitely did not want their parents along on a Pee Wee trip.

"That's too bad," said Mary Beth.

"She should be working," said Molly crossly.

Mrs. Peters was telling the Pee Wees what to pack and how to behave. She was telling them about manners and that there would be no running or shouting on the train or in the hotel. Usually Molly would be making a list. But this time she wasn't even listening. After all, her mother would pack for her. And she surely wouldn't run and shout with her mother nearby. She wouldn't be able to do anything that was any fun.

On the way home Molly tried to think of ways to make her mother change her mind. Wasn't her mother too old to travel with a lot of rowdy children? And who would keep her dad company? Had her mom thought of that? What if Molly's

grandma got sick or Mrs. Duff was needed at work in an emergency?

When Molly got home, she said, "I don't think we should leave Dad alone for a whole weekend. He'll get lonesome."

"He'd have plenty to do," said Mrs.

Duff. "But guess what? Dad is invited to come with us! After your meeting today Mr. Peters called to say he's coming, and he wants Dad to join him. Isn't that great?"

Rat's knees. Now she had two parents to ruin her trip instead of one! Why had she even mentioned it? Still, it wasn't Molly who had made her dad come. It was Mr. Peters, and it had been arranged before Molly even asked.

"Just in case you don't really want to come, Jody's mom and Rachel's mom could come," said Molly in a last-ditch effort to save the trip.

"We wouldn't miss it for the world," said her mom. "But it almost sounds like you don't *want* us along!"

"I do," lied Molly. Sometimes it was just not polite to tell the truth. She didn't want to hurt her parents' feelings.

"We won't treat you any differently

than anyone else on the trip," said her mother. "We'll just ignore you. In fact, with Roger and Sonny there, I think we'll have plenty to do keeping an eye on them to be sure they aren't getting into trouble."

Molly smiled. It was true that some of the Pee Wees needed more watching than others.

The phone rang. It was Tracy. "Too bad about your mom," she said.

"Not only my mom," groaned Molly. "My dad is coming too."

"Bad luck," said Tracy. "My mom couldn't get off work even if she wanted to."

"She must have a good job," said Molly.

Well, there was no use crying over spilled milk, as Molly's grandma always said. She would have to be brave and try to make the best of the ruined trip.

CHAPTER 4

Lost and Found

"Departing on track seven," said a deep, gravelly voice that sounded to Molly as if it were coming from the bottom of a pit. "Track seven," it repeated, "for Smoky Junction, Argyle, Rochester, and Center City."

"That's us!" shouted Sonny, running toward track seven. "That's our train!"

"There's no rush," said Mr. Duff. He pointed to the sign that was lit up over the ticket windows. "The timetable says it leaves at nine-oh-four. We have plenty of time. And I'd like to get a cup of coffee first."

"We'll miss the train!" shouted Sonny. "The guy said it's reporting!"

Rachel rolled her eyes. "That's *departing*," she told him. "And trains can't leave before it says on the sign. It's a law."

Rachel knew a lot. Molly had learned many things from her. Like where silverware and napkins went when you set the table. And how to get grape juice out of a new sweater your grandma knitted before your mom could see the stain. And now something else she'd never known. Trains could not leave before the time it said on the sign. No matter what.

Sonny looked as if he did not believe Rachel. He went over to the door to track seven and sat down on his backpack.

"Let's all have a look at the model rail-road set up over here," said Mrs. Peters in her Scout leader voice. Molly's mother herded the Pee Wees along, and Mr. Peters guided Sonny forward with the rest.

"The train is leaving!" said Sonny. "It's going without us!"

"Baby," said Tracy.

"We'll just have a look at the model trains and then we'll go," said Mrs. Peters. "See, there isn't even a line in front of track seven yet."

The man in charge of the model rail-road was glad to have an audience. The Pee Wees watched as a little model train went up hills and down valleys and across bridges. It stopped at the little train station in the make-believe town. It stopped while the engineer switched tracks to let another train pass.

"Isn't it cute!" said Lisa. "Look, there

are even little tables in the dining car!"

"Hey, is there real oil in those tank cars?" shouted Roger.

"What a dumb question," said Mary Beth. "Of course there isn't real oil. That would be dangerous."

The man didn't call Roger dumb; he just said no. He told the Pee Wees how important trains were for carrying freight. "They carried lumber from the mills and coal from the mines," he said.

"Now they carry brand-new cars," said Tim. "The car my uncle just bought came on a train."

"Let's go," whined Sonny, who wasn't paying attention to the model trains. He was looking toward the real train that had pulled in on track seven. A small crowd was beginning to gather in front of the door that led to the track.

The Pee Wees thanked the man and

followed the Peterses to the rest rooms. When they came out, Mr. Peters and Mr. Duff made sure each Scout had their own backpack or overnight bag. They made sure they knew how to fold Jody's wheel-chair to get it on the train.

"Well, I guess we can go to track seven and line up," said Mrs. Peters. She began to count noses. She counted several times, Molly thought. Their leader frowned. She went to talk to Mrs. Duff.

All four adults looked around.

"Someone's missing," said Kenny.

"Who?" asked Jody.

"Well, it's not Roger. Darn," said Mary Beth. Roger was running and sliding on the marble floor and making faces at a baby in a stroller.

"It's Sonny," said Mrs. Peters. "Have any of you seen Sonny since we came out of the rest rooms?"

The Pee Wees looked around. Sonny was not with the group. He was not at the door to track seven with the crowd. And he was not running and sliding with Roger.

Mr. Duff ran back to the model trains and spoke to the man. Molly could see him describing Sonny and holding his hand up to show how tall he was. But the man shook his head.

Now the crowd at the door to track seven was getting bigger. The light went on over the door, and the man in charge opened the door and began to check tickets.

"Stay here and don't move," said Mrs. Peters to the Scouts as the four adults went to search.

"Rat's knees, we *are* going to miss the train!" said Molly, watching as the people began to walk through the door, along the platform, and onto the train.

"Last call for Smoky Junction, Argyle,

Rochester, and Center City," called the deep, gravelly voice. "Track seven."

Now all the Pee Wees were anxious, except Roger. He was begging Jody for a ride in his wheelchair.

As the last passenger went through the door, the Duffs and Peterses returned— without Sonny. Suddenly the deep voice of the announcer came on again. "Will Sonny Stone please come to track seven," he said. "Sonny Stone, track seven."

"He can't have gone far in just a few minutes," said Mr. Duff, trying to reassure everyone.

"He'll be here in a minute when he hears that announcement," said Mr. Peters. "After all, he was the one who was afraid of being late."

The Pee Wees heard a loud train whistle. They heard wheels turning. Then, through the open door, they saw their train pull out of the station. And pressed against the back train window, looking back at them, Molly saw a familiar face. It was Sonny!

CHAPTER

All Aboard . . . Finally

"**S**onny is on that train!" shouted Molly. Everyone looked where she pointed. The train was moving slowly out of the station.

Mr. Duff and Mr. Peters dashed through the door and out to the track. It was too late. The train was gone, and Sonny was on it.

Mrs. Peters ran to the desk and explained what had happened.

"He's too young to travel alone!" she cried.

"Don't worry," a man in a railroad uniform reassured them. "These things happen all the time."

"All the time?" asked Mrs. Duff.

"Well, every once in a while," the man said. "We'll just call ahead, and you can meet him at Smoky Junction. He'll be perfectly safe. He's probably pretty worried by now, but we know how to handle these things."

While the Peterses were thanking the man, the Pee Wees were muttering.

"Special care, that's what Sonny needs full-time," said Tracy in disgust. "He can't be trusted away from his mother."

"He can't be trusted *with* his mother," said Lisa. "He's such a baby."

"Now, you folks will have to take the next train out of here for Smoky Junction, and it doesn't leave until . . ." The man ran his finger down the schedule. "Until noon."

The Pee Wees groaned. Three hours to wait because they'd missed the train that Sonny was on. What was worse, that meant three hours in the train station with Roger.

The adults looked relieved, thought Molly, but Mrs. Peters's lips were narrow, the way they got at meetings when there was trouble—when she'd "had enough."

"How did he get on without a ticket?" asked Kevin.

"How did he get through the door when it was closed?" asked Jody.

"Now we're going to get to Center City late," said Rachel. "And miss lots of stuff. Our whole weekend will be gone before we even get there."

But Mr. Duff cheered everyone up by starting some word games. They played

I Spy, and Molly won. She was used to playing that game in the car on trips with her grandma.

Kevin won Twenty Questions. "Your dad's a lot of fun!" he said.

Molly felt good for a moment that her father had come. Kevin liked him! And he was right, Mr. Duff was a lot of fun. And her mother had not done anything embarrassing yet. Maybe having her parents along wouldn't be as bad as she'd imagined.

The time finally passed, and the Pee Wees got on the train. When it stopped at Smoky Junction, a conductor swung Sonny aboard. Sonny was eating a candy bar and drinking a can of soda pop. He had an engineer's cap on his head and did not look upset about having been alone on the train.

"Hey, you guys, I told you you'd miss the train! I was the only one that didn't."

Mrs. Peters had a wild look in her eye. Molly thought she looked as if she'd shake Sonny if it were legal.

"I got to sit with the engineer," said Sonny. "This is really a fun trip."

"For *you*, maybe," said Kenny.

"You are so selfish," said Rachel.

It did not seem to Molly that Sonny should be rewarded for being a big baby, but he was. He was the center of attention too, which was just what he liked.

"I knew you guys were going to miss the train. I told you so," said Sonny. "So I snuck down to the tracks through another door and got on the train early. Do you know they don't ask for your ticket until the middle of the trip?"

Mrs. Peters and Molly's mother took Sonny aside and talked to him quietly. Sonny was not smiling as much when they finished.

"I'm hungry," said Roger. The other Pee Wees said they were hungry too.

"We're lucky that the dining car will serve us all lunch this late in the day," said Mr. Duff. He started on the trek between cars, on his way to feed the hungry brood.

CHAPTER 6

First Stop:
The Ritz

"Center City!" called the conductor, walking through the train. "Next stop, Center City!"

Passengers scrambled to get their bags together. Molly could see buses and taxicabs and cars from the train window. It felt exciting!

"This is a big city," she said to Mary Beth.

Mary Beth agreed.

39

"This is small compared to New York, where my cousin lives," said Rachel. "You should see the museums they have there! I'll bet they have a million."

Inside the station, Mr. and Mrs. Peters walked ahead of the Pee Wees. The Duffs walked behind them, to be sure that no one wandered off.

"Where are we going first, Mrs. Peters?" asked Patty when they were all standing out on the noisy street.

"To the Ritz Hotel," said their leader. "When we get there, I'll tell you our itinerary."

"What's a tinnery?" asked Sonny.

"A place where they make tin cans, dummy," said Roger.

Rachel looked disgusted. "That's *itinerary.* It's a travel plan," she said.

At the Ritz men and women with briefcases were pushing in and out through revolving doors. Molly could see people eating and drinking in a fancy restaurant that had one whole wall of glass windows. The diners all seemed to be laughing and talking and having a good time.

"This is a fancy place!" said Kenny, looking across the huge lobby. It had a grand piano in the middle and lots of tall potted plants and trees.

"When you walk on this rug, you sink into it!" said Tim.

"How can those trees grow inside?" asked Lisa. "And what happens when they touch the roof?"

Mr. Peters and Mr. Duff checked everyone in. They had to have several rooms for a group the size of the Pee Wees.

On the elevator a woman in a red velvet dress carried a little dog wearing a

red coat and matching red boots.

"Those are mother-daughter outfits," whispered Tracy.

"I'll bet they're in the circus," said Roger. Mrs. Peters frowned at him.

When they got to their rooms, Molly was relieved to find that she didn't have to spend the night in the same room as her parents, or worse, Roger. Mr. Duff and Mr. Peters were in charge of the boys. And in Molly's room, Mrs. Peters took charge of half the girls. Mrs. Duff stayed in another room with the rest of the girls.

Having her parents on the trip was not so bad, thought Molly. It appeared she had worried for nothing. So far her parents had caused no trouble or embarrassment, and in fact all the Pee Wees seemed to be entertained by her father.

In the first room, the Pee Wees found more things to do and see. There were big, bouncy beds, little bars of soap and bottles of shampoo, and a real hair dryer built right into the wall.

"That way no one can steal it," said Rachel.

"Hey, look at the little refrigerator!" shouted Sonny. "It's filled with candy and stuff!"

"You have to pay for what you take out," warned Jody. "It's not free."

After all the bags were in the right rooms, Mrs. Peters tried to get the Pee Wees to be quiet so that she could discuss the plans. But they were so wound up with excitement, no one could listen.

"Even though we got a late start," said Mrs. Peters above the noise, looking at Sonny, "we are going to the museum. Because of our delay, we have to get a move on. The museum is a large place, and it will take at least two trips to see it all."

The Pee Wees moaned. "Can't we stay here?" said Sonny. "Can't we go exploring in the hotel?"

"There's a swimming pool on the tenth floor, Mrs. Peters," said Rachel. "I think we should take advantage of it. It comes with the rooms."

Mrs. Peters looked a little tired, Molly thought.

"We didn't come here to see the hotel, boys and girls! We came here to see things of historical interest—things we can't see at home."

The Pee Wees groaned. The museum had sounded like fun when they were at home. But now it didn't seem as much fun as exploring the hotel and going swimming on the tenth floor, high above Center City.

"We can't see a hotel like this at home!" shouted Sonny. "I think for my badge I'll draw a picture of the swimming pool!"

"Forget the museum!" exclaimed Roger. "There's a TV in the lobby with a screen as big as a movie theater! And Spider-Man was on!"

The boys cheered and started toward the door. But Mr. Duff stopped them and herded them back. "TV is something we have at home," he said. "And no one gets a badge for drawing a picture of the swimming pool!"

Molly began to see why they had to have four adults along on this trip.

"We have no time to waste. We have to get to the museum right away," said Mrs. Peters.

All the other Pee Wees looked at Sonny. It was his fault they couldn't have a swim or go exploring in the hotel. But Sonny didn't look as if it bothered him at all.

Everyone began to get ready to go to the museum. They used the bathroom and brushed their hair and washed their hands and faces. They got back on the elevator while Mr. Duff studied the city map.

"These elevators tickle my stomach!" said Molly.

"Mine too," said Mary Beth.

When they got off in the lobby, Tim said, "Hey, look at that guy over there." He pointed to a sofa partly concealed by a flowering bush.

"What about him?" asked Patty.

"He looks suspicious," said Tim. "He's got shifty eyes and a tattoo of a snake on his arm."

"My cousin's got a tattoo," said Lisa. "And he's no crook."

"Lots of people have tattoos," said Kevin. "My uncle's got one and he's nice."

But Tim was not convinced.

Molly agreed with Tim. This man could be dangerous. He had a hat on, even inside the hotel. Almost no men wore hats. Maybe this guy was staking out the hotel. What if he was the leader of a band of criminals? Would the Pee Wees be in danger? Molly could save them!

Then Molly remembered her wild imagination. It was running away with her again. Her imagination often got her into trouble.

Anyway, that man was probably someone's uncle. Or a dentist or a doctor or a bus driver or even a policeman!

"He's trouble," said Tim. "I'm telling you now, that guy's a crook!"

CHAPTER 7

Mummies
(but No Daddies)

"**H**e's probably an FBI agent or something," said Jody.

"Or maybe he's a regular guy," said Rachel. "A boxer or a wrestler."

But even allowing for her imagination, Molly thought Tim might be right. Tim wasn't exactly a fortune-teller, but he often knew about things that were going to happen before the other Pee Wees did. He knew what people were like just by looking at them. It was a talent.

As they passed the man on the way out, Molly could see that Tim's crook looked nervous. His hands were shaking, and he seemed to be blushing as if someone had caught him doing something bad.

As the Pee Wees passed him he put his newspaper in front of his face. Molly had the feeling he was just pretending to read. She had the feeling he was hiding. But from what?

The Pee Wees climbed onto a city bus and rode for blocks. There was a lot to see in Center City. Molly felt as if she could write ten papers about what she saw. But if she wanted her badge, she had to write about what she saw in the museum.

The Pee Wees got off the bus in front of a large building with statues on either side of the front doors. Big letters overhead said SCIENCE AND HISTORY MUSEUM. In the huge lobby full of echoes a guard in a uniform smiled at them.

Mr. Duff asked a few questions at the main desk and then led everyone to a room that had ancient treasures in it. There were pieces of broken dishes with colors still bright on them and cave paintings done with berry juice.

"This tells us a bit about how people lived thousands of years ago," said Mr. Duff.

"Why did they use such old stuff?" asked Sonny. "Couldn't they afford to get stuff that wasn't all cracked up?"

Mary Beth rolled her eyes at Molly. "He is so dumb," she said.

Mrs. Peters was patient and explained to Sonny and the others that when these people had lived, these things had been new. There were no department stores or discount stores to shop in. "They had to make their own dishes out of clay from the earth," she said. "These people lived a very, very long time ago."

Molly studied the treasures and found it hard to believe anything could be that old.

"And here is the exhibit of mummies," said Mrs. Duff, reading the sign that told how the ancient people preserved the bodies. There were rows of mummies, wrapped in white cloths and lying in fancy decorated boxes.

"That's a real person!" said Jody. "Just think of that!"

The Pee Wees did think. There was a lot to think about here.

"Mrs. Peters," said Lisa, "why did they preserve the mummies and not the daddies?"

Mrs. Peters smiled at the question. Molly didn't know why she was smiling. It was a good question—one Molly had wanted to ask herself. Why did you have to be a mother in order to be preserved?

"Mummies are not necessarily mommies," said their leader.

This was not very clear. The Pee Wees frowned.

"That is, some mommies did become mummies, but so did some daddies. We don't know for sure if these mummies are men or women."

"You can't be a mommy if you're a man," said Tracy firmly.

Mrs. Peters explained that *mummy* did not mean "mother." It meant a body that had been preserved after death by being wrapped in cloths and herbs and other solutions. "After a while, it becomes mummified," she said.

"It's spooky!" said Patty. "Think how old they are!"

"Where did the mummies and the

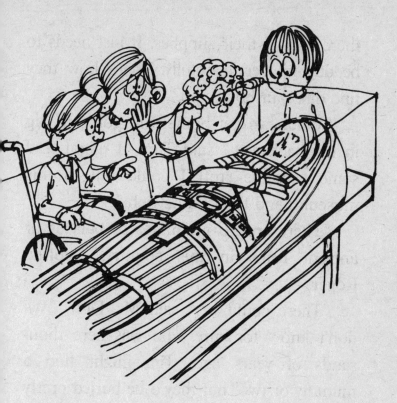

treasures come from, Mrs. Peters?" asked Tim.

"That's a good question, Tim," said Mrs. Peters. "Men and women called archaeologists dig through ancient ruins to find them. They have found palaces and whole buried cities complete with the people who lived there and all their supplies. It just needs to be dug up very carefully. That's how they find dinosaur bones too."

"When we get home, I'm going to dig in my backyard," said Tim. "I might find some valuable stuff I could sell to this museum, and then I'd be rich."

"There are no mummies or palaces or ancient ruins in this country," scoffed Roger.

"There could be," said Mr. Duff. "We don't know for sure who was here thousands of years ago. Tim might find a mummy or two, but they'd be buried pretty deep. He'd need a pretty big shovel!"

"Mrs. Peters, I'm hungry!" said Sonny.

The other Pee Wees groaned. "How can he think of food when we're looking at these old dead mummies?" asked Mary Beth.

"Well," said Mrs. Peters, looking at her

watch, "we can get you something at the snack bar downstairs, and then we'll have to move on to the dinosaur room. Time is flying."

When they got to the snack bar, they all stood in line. Sonny got a hot dog, and the others had soda pop.

"How do you know that hot dog didn't come from some old tomb?" said Roger to Sonny. "It could be a million years old!"

"They didn't have hot dogs a million years ago," said Rachel. "Anyone who knows history knows that."

Roger made a face at Rachel.

On the way out of the snack bar, Molly noticed a man leaning against the pop machine. He was reading a newspaper. He looked familiar.

"It's him!" whispered Tim to Molly. "Look! It's the crook with the shifty eyes from the hotel!"

CHAPTER 8

A Fake Dinosaur

"**W**hat's he doing here?" said Tracy.

"He's probably just sightseeing like we are," said Mrs. Peters when Tim told her about the man.

"He's not a Pee Wee Scout," said Tim. "And he isn't here to sightsee. He's a crook."

"You can't go around calling everyone a crook just because you don't like the way they look," said Rachel to Tim.

Rachel was right, thought Molly. And yet . . . she trusted Tim's feeling. She was more and more convinced the man was no one's kind old uncle.

The Pee Wees followed the Peterses and the Duffs into the dinosaur hall. Molly tried to forget about the man. If he was a troublemaker, the adults would handle it. That was their job.

In the middle of the room stood a huge dinosaur skeleton. A sign said it was a *Tyrannosaurus rex* and explained its size and where it had lived and what kind of food it had eaten.

"Hey, where's his skin?" shouted Roger. "He's nothing but bones!"

"This is a model," said Mr. Duff. "These are man-made bones created in the exact size and shape of the real thing."

"Are the mummies man-made too?"

asked Kevin in a disappointed voice.

"No," said Mr. Duff. "The Egyptian artifacts are real."

"This claw is the real thing," said a woman attendant next to a glass case. "This is the claw of a real *Apatosaurus* that lived more than a million years ago."

The Pee Wees gathered around the glass case. There, on a little platform inside the case, rested the claw. A real claw was better than a whole fake dinosaur, thought Molly.

"That's right out of some old dead dinosaur's foot," said Tracy in amazement.

It was about four inches long. It looked sharp.

"Wow!" said Kevin. "That must be very valuable."

"It is," said the attendant.

"Do you know what?" said Tim. "Dinosaurs lived on earth longer than human beings have been here."

"Really?" said Mrs. Duff.

The attendant nodded. "He's right," she said. "We often think of them as dumb animals because they had such large bodies and such small heads, but they were very smart."

"Tim knows more than we think," said Mary Beth to Molly.

Molly nodded. "About a lot of things," she said, thinking of the man from the hotel lobby.

"Can we touch the claw?" asked Patty.

"I'm afraid not," said the attendant. "We can't remove the artifacts and fossils from the cases. They could get broken or even stolen. I'm sorry."

The children studied the claw some more and then moved on to an exhibit of Egyptian jewelry.

"Look at that!" said Kenny, pointing at

something very sparkly on a red velvet cushion. The cushion was on a big table, and the table was inside a big glass case.

"That's the prize of our collection," said the attendant. "It's a gold necklace worn by an Egyptian queen. It's our most valuable treasure."

The Pee Wees gazed at the necklace. It was a large, round ring of gold with gold loops hanging from it. On each loop were three precious stones. Molly closed her eyes and tried to picture an ancient Egyptian queen wearing it around her neck.

"Hey, my aunt has one of those," said Roger.

"She does not," said Rachel. "There's only one like it in the entire world."

"I'd like to give one of those to my mom for Mother's Day," said Tim. "She'd like it."

"If she had one, she'd be the richest

person in the world," said Kevin.

"If she had that one, she couldn't wear it," said Jody. "Someone would steal it. She'd have to put it in the bank and wear a fake one."

The Pee Wees moved on to an exhibit of Greek urns. From there they went to look at more pictures that had been scratched onto cave walls.

"I don't know what to write about to earn my badge," said Lisa. "There are so many things."

"The necklace would be fun to draw," said Mary Beth. "I'll bet everybody draws that or writes about it. Or maybe the genuine dinosaur claw."

Molly hadn't made up her mind what to write about, but she took notes in her little notebook at every exhibit. That way she would have information. She could decide later what to write about.

When a voice on the loudspeaker announced closing time at the museum, the Pee Wees moaned.

"We'll come back tomorrow," said Mrs. Peters, leading them toward an exit.

On the way out, Tim poked Molly. "Look!" he said.

Tim was pointing to the case where the necklace had been. The cushion was still there, but the necklace was gone! The door of the case was wide open!

And standing nearby, putting something into his coat pocket, was the man from the hotel.

By Hook or by Crook

As Molly and Tim watched, the man walked rapidly out the door.

"Did you see that?" yelled Tim. "The necklace is gone! And so is that guy!"

But it was too late to do anything. They had to get out of the building with the others. And when they did, the man was nowhere in sight.

On the way home, Molly and Tim told everyone what they had seen.

"We have to be very careful not to let our imaginations run away with us," said Molly's mother. Her mother was starting to act like her mother again, thought Molly.

"Sometimes Molly can't tell the difference between storytelling and reality," said Mr. Duff, laughing.

Now it came back to her why she had not wanted her parents along on this trip. I may have a wild imagination, thought Molly, but I know what I saw.

"Tim saw it too!" said Molly.

"It's easy to be swept up in all the excitement," said Mrs. Peters, "and see things that aren't really there."

Rat's knees, thought Molly. Now Mrs. Peters is doing it too!

"We have to be careful not to judge others rashly," Mrs. Peters went on.

What did this have to do with a rash?

thought Molly. This wasn't a time to discuss rashes. This was a crime the police should handle!

"We have to get this guy," Tim whispered to Molly. "We have to find him, by hook or by crook. He's probably back at our hotel. That's where he's staying."

But back at the hotel, things were quiet. There was no sign of the man. And of course Molly and Tim didn't know his name. No one was looking for crooks. People were getting ready for dinner. Soft music was playing in the lobby, and the rest of the Pee Wees wanted to go for a swim.

Maybe her mother was right—maybe Molly had been overexcited. How could a crook be staying in this nice, quiet, fancy hotel? She was being silly about the whole thing.

The Scouts headed for the pool. It was

big, and the water was very, very blue.

"Here I go!" shouted Roger, holding his nose and jumping off the edge with a big splash.

"It smells funny," said Mary Beth.

"That's the chlorine," said Rachel. "It kills germs."

"Maybe I'll write about this pool to get my badge," said Tim. "It might be old."

"Ha, like one year old!" said Roger. "This pool's not historical."

"No, but I wish you were," said Rachel as Roger tried to duck her head under the water.

All the Pee Wees laughed except Roger. They swam and played water games, and then took showers and went back to their rooms and got dressed for dinner.

"I hope they have hamburgers and not just all that green salad stuff. I hate vegetables," said Roger.

"I'll bet vegetables hate him too!" whispered Mary Beth.

On the way to the dining room they went through the lobby. The TV was on, and Molly caught a glimpse of the picture. It looked like the museum where they had been that afternoon!

"Hey, what did that guy say about the museum?" asked Tim. "I heard him. He said something about that necklace!"

"Maybe he said it was stolen," said Sonny. "That would be on the news because it's so valuable. They probably want help finding the thief."

"I told you so!" said Tim. "I told you that guy in our hotel stole it."

Mr. Duff frowned. "Even if you're right, you need proof. To accuse someone of a crime, you have to have proof. And we don't have any. Let's just leave that up to the police."

Molly wished she could tell the police what she had seen. But her dad was right, as usual. You couldn't point fingers and tell on someone without proof. Even if you were sure he did it. It was the law.

"I think we should scout around and explore the hotel for clues," Tim said to

Molly. "We have to find real proof to back us up. And we have to do it fast, before the guy gets away."

Tim was right. There was no time to waste. In a way it was their duty. It was what Scouting was all about: helping others, doing good deeds. And if they caught a thief, it would be one giant good deed! Molly couldn't wait to finish dinner and start collecting evidence.

Then, before they knew what was happening, the evidence came to them.

CHAPTER 10

A Dog Named Roger

Just as the Pee Wees were served their chocolate sundaes, the crook walked in. He was with the woman the Pee Wees had seen on the elevator—the woman who was dressed like her dog. They sat down together and ordered dinner. The little dog sat on the man's lap.

"I wonder if they're married," said Mary Beth. "Maybe she's Mrs. Crook."

While the couple waited for their dinner, the dog began to growl and dig in the man's pocket.

"Bad dog, Roger!" cried the woman.

"Hey, the dog is named after you, Roger!" shouted Sonny, pointing. All the Pee Wees began to laugh. Roger turned red and looked embarrassed.

The man tried to pull Roger the dog away from his pocket, but it was too late. Roger had dug his little feet and nose firmly in and was now pulling something out of the pocket. It looked like a jewelry box! A long jewelry box that could hold a necklace! *The* necklace! Here it was, right in front of them, thought Molly. Evidence, proof! And it had come right to them. It must be a sign that they were on the right track.

"Get him!" shouted Tim, standing up and tipping over his chair. "Roger found the proof we need! That's the missing necklace!"

The Peterses and the Duffs tried to calm the Pee Wees down. But it was too late. With Tim in the lead, the rest of the Pee Wees raced over to the man's table. Molly wondered what they would do when they got there. Could the Pee Wees really capture the thief and tie him up? But no one had thought to bring any rope!

Roger the dog got excited and bounced to the floor, and when the thief stood up, he tripped over the dog and fell.

"Get him!" shouted Tim again.

"Poor Roger!" cried Mrs. Crook, scooping her dog into her arms. "Are you hurt?"

"She seems more worried about the dog than about her husband," murmured Mary Beth to Molly.

"Unless he isn't her husband," said Molly.

When the man looked up from where

he'd fallen, he saw that he was surrounded by twelve Pee Wee Scouts, all glaring down at him. Twenty-four eyes stared at a hairy face and two shifty eyes.

By now the Duffs and Peterses had arrived at the table. They began to apologize and pull the Pee Wees away. The noise had attracted the waiters and the hotel manager.

"Nothing like this has ever happened before," said the manager, wringing his hands. "Are you hurt, Mr. Ross?" He looked at the Pee Wees. "Why are you doing this to Mr. Ross?"

"This man just robbed the museum. It was on the news, and we saw him," said Kevin.

All of a sudden Mr. Ross began to laugh. He lay on the floor and laughed and laughed and laughed. Finally he got to his feet and brushed himself off. Then he held his hands up over his head.

"He's surrendering," whispered Mary Beth to Molly. "That's what criminals on TV do when they've been caught."

But Mr. Ross was not surrendering. Still laughing, he said, "I'm no crook. I'm an actor. I was at the museum studying Egyptian customs and decoration. I'm in a historical play, and this is the leading lady, Betsy Wright." Mr. Ross motioned toward Roger the dog's owner. "I was hoping Betsy would become my wife. I was just about to present her with this engagement gift, a gold necklace, when you all descended on us like a swarm of hornets!"

The Pee Wees were speechless. This might be the most embarrassing thing they had ever done as a group, thought Molly. She was sure people were arrested for things like this.

"Not so fast," said Roger. "You may be

a fast talker, but how do we know you aren't the crook? Maybe you're lying. Maybe you're a con man. Let's see that necklace."

Leave it to Roger to make a bad situation worse, thought Molly. Mr. Peters and Mr. Duff quickly took Roger aside and held on to him while they gave him a private lecture.

"What in the world can we do to make up for this?" Mrs. Peters was saying to Mr. Ross. She was straightening the tablecloth.

"The manager might throw us all out of the hotel," said Mary Beth worriedly. "I just hope it's not on the news tonight, or in the newspaper: 'Pee Wee Scouts Cause Trouble in Center City.'"

Mr. Ross was very kind about the mistake, but the hotel manager did not look pleased.

"The Scouts meant well," said Mr. Ross. "After all, it is a good thing for them to try to rid the city of crime."

"I think we have learned a valuable lesson here," said Mr. Duff. "We must not jump to conclusions, and if there is trouble, it is best to let the authorities handle it. It is not good to take matters into our own hands."

Mr. Duff glared at Tim and Roger. Molly felt just as much at fault. After all, she had trusted Tim's feeling. Tim had been right so often. But it just proved that no one was right all the time. Molly would have to write that down in her notebook and remember it.

Mrs. Duff picked up the gift box that had fallen onto the floor. She brushed it off and set it on the table. "I can't tell you how sorry we are," she said. "And now I think we should just get out of your way and let you try to go on with your dinner and your evening."

"I think you should all join us," said Mr. Ross. "It would be more festive that way. It will be an evening Betsy and I will never forget."

"And Roger," said Sonny. "He won't forget it either."

Now everyone was laughing. Mr. Ross ordered another dessert for all the Pee Wees because their sundaes had melted. Then he handed Betsy the gift box with teeth marks in it. "Will you marry me?" he asked.

Betsy leaned over, gave Mr. Ross a kiss, and said, "Of course I will."

Tracy and Lisa had tears in their eyes. "It's just like in a play or a movie," said Lisa.

The necklace that Mr. Ross fastened

around Betsy's neck was gold, but it was
not the museum necklace. It was smaller
and had gold links and one little diamond
hanging in the middle.

"It's wonderful!" said Betsy. "And I'll remember this night always."

Then the Pee Wees dug into their dessert.

"I wonder who really did take the necklace at the museum," said Tim.

"I don't think anyone did," said Mr. Ross.

"But it was gone," said Molly.

"Maybe they took it out to clean it," said Betsy.

"But it was on TV," said Tim.

"That was just an announcement about some new artifacts that arrived at the museum," said Mr. Ross. "I saw that on the way into the dining room."

The Pee Wees groaned. It seemed to Molly they hadn't been right about anything on this trip!

CHAPTER 11

Betsy Ross

"I wonder why Roger the dog tried to get that box out of your pocket," said Kevin to Mr. Ross.

"Well, it is sort of bone-shaped," said Betsy. "And it made a bulge in his pocket that probably attracted Roger's attention. He's a curious dog, and he probably had to find out what it was."

Finally, after more apologies from the Duffs and the Peterses and the Pee Wees, they all went to their rooms and left the couple to celebrate their engagement in peace.

On the elevator, Mr. Peters told the Pee Wees, "We're lucky that Mr. Ross didn't press charges. This whole incident could have been much worse."

The Pee Wees hung their heads. They realized they were lucky. They deserved some kind of awful punishment, Molly knew.

"I think all of you have learned a lesson here," said Mrs. Duff. "You don't need any punishment to help you remember."

Her mother was reading her mind. Something like the way Molly had read Tim's. But of course Molly had been wrong. This time, anyway.

"Hey," said Jody, wheeling down the hotel hallway. "If Betsy marries Mr. Ross, she'll become Betsy Ross!"

Most of the Pee Wees looked puzzled. Lisa said, "So what?"

"Betsy Ross made the first flag," said Kevin.

"I knew that," said Rachel.

"So did I," said Mary Beth.

"Hey, they should get married on Flag Day!" said Roger.

"She should have a red-white-and-blue dress!" said Tracy.

"Or a cake in the shape of a flag!" said Molly.

"They could decorate it with stars and stripes," said Patty.

"A lot of women don't take the man's name anymore," said Rachel. "I'll bet Betsy will just stay Betsy Wright."

That ended the Pee Wees' wedding talk. There were no funny Betsy Wright stories. And no historical stories about that name.

Mrs. Peters clapped her hands together and said, "Tomorrow is a big day. We have to see the rest of the museum and then come back here and pack up and get the train to go home. Right now we all need a good night's sleep."

Most of the Pee Wees were yawning. It had been a full day. A lot had happened, thought Molly. Trains and museums and bones and necklaces and mistaken identity. No matter what tomorrow brought, it couldn't be as eventful as today had been.

Molly slept soundly and didn't wake up until the sun came streaming through the hotel window. The sun looked brighter and seemed to rise earlier here in Center City than at home.

Before long there was a noise in the hall. It was Roger chasing Sonny with a rubber spider he had bought in the gift shop at the museum.

"When do we eat?" asked Sonny when Mrs. Duff put the spider in her pocket.

"Right now," said Mrs. Peters. "Let's get down to the dining room before the rush."

When the Pee Wees were seated, they noticed Mr. Ross and Betsy across the room. They waved. It was hard to believe that the scene the night before had really happened, thought Molly. Everyone looked so respectable in the morning. Even Mr. Ross, who had looked like a crook just yesterday. Molly wondered why they had ever thought he was a crook. He still had the hat and the tattoo, but he did not look sinister. He looked like a nice, friendly man eating breakfast.

Sonny and Roger each ate six pancakes and then wanted more.

Mr. Peters shook his head. "We have a lot to do and see today," he said. "And all those pancakes will slow you down."

"That's disgusting," said Mary Beth to Molly. "Those pancakes are as big as Frisbees."

When everyone had finished breakfast, Troop 23 set off for the museum. This time they went to rooms they had not seen the day before. They saw treasures from a shipwreck, an airplane flown by the Wright brothers (no relation to Betsy, Mr. Duff was sure), Native American ceremonial costumes and jewelry, and even a live baby shark swimming in a big tank.

The morning flew by, and after lunch in the museum's cafeteria there was talk about checking out of the hotel and getting to the train station on time.

On the way out of the museum, the Pee Wees walked past the room with the Egyptian jewelry in it. Tim was heading for the gift shop to get his own rubber spider and seemed to have forgotten all about the missing necklace.

"Hey," said Kevin to Molly. "Let's go in and see if the necklace is back."

They walked toward the big case. In the case was the velvet pillow, and on the pillow was the necklace! It looked exactly as it had before—as if it had never gone anywhere.

"Maybe we did imagine it was gone," said Molly.

Kevin shook his head. "It was gone," he said. "But I guess it wasn't stolen."

A new attendant smiled at Molly and Kevin. "This just got back," she said, nodding. "It was gone for cleaning and polishing yesterday."

Molly felt relieved. There was no thief involved, but it hadn't been her wild imagination playing tricks on her! The necklace really had been gone for cleaning, just as Betsy had suggested.

When the Pee Wees got back to the hotel, Mr. Peters suggested they take a little nap while the adults packed, so that no one would be overtired and irritable on the trip home.

"Like Sonny and Roger," whispered Mary Beth to Molly. "They're the only babies that need a nap."

Molly couldn't sleep. Now that the trip was almost over, all she could think about was choosing her favorite thing in the museum to write about. She had so many favorite things! She could write a paper about each one of them.

"What are you going to write about?" she whispered to Mary Beth, who wasn't sleeping either.

"The baby shark, I think," Mary Beth said. "Probably no one else will choose him. I like his name, Scamper."

Soon the Pee Wees had checked out of the hotel and were headed toward the train station. The adults kept a sharp eye on Sonny this time, and they all got on the right train together. There was a lot of conversation about what they had seen on the trip, but Molly curled up on her seat and closed her eyes. She liked to think about good times by herself and remember what she had done and how she had felt. That was even more fun than talking about it.

And then, before long, the trip was over and the Pee Wees were home.

CHAPTER 12

Molly's Imagination Pays Off

"**R**emember," said Mrs. Peters as the Pee Wees got off the train and into their parents' waiting cars, "have your papers and pictures ready by Tuesday! Tuesday is badge day!"

Molly's mind was spinning. Maybe she should write about the necklace. But many of the Pee Wees would choose that, she thought. She wanted something different.

The shark? That was Mary Beth's choice. She didn't want to be a copycat.

The mummies? Too grisly. Dead bodies were no fun.

In the morning Molly woke up with an idea. Morning ideas were always good. She had a perfect thing to write about. The only problem was, how could she get it all on one sheet of paper? She would have to write very, very small. Perhaps she could use the other side of the paper too. Mrs. Peters had said one sheet of paper. But she hadn't said they couldn't use both sides of it!

At school, all the Pee Wees were talking about their badge project.

"I'm going to do the dinosaur claw," said Kenny.

"I'm going to write about those dishes that were in the shipwreck," said Rachel.

"I don't think anyone else noticed them."

But Molly didn't talk about her project. She was sure her subject wouldn't be chosen by anyone else. She wrote before breakfast and after lunch. At school and after school. Her project was too long. Molly took lots of words out. Then it was too short. She put some of the words back in. Then she copied it over in very small writing on both sides of one sheet of paper. It had been so much fun writing it, she was sorry to be finished.

On Tuesday the Pee Wees gathered in the Peterses' basement. Mrs. Peters had a pile of badges in front of her.

"I think we should all read our papers out loud to the group," she said. "That way we can all enjoy them! And if you drew a picture, you can hold it up when it's your turn."

Sonny held his picture up first. It was the dinosaur claw.

"Darn!" said Tim. "I drew that too!"

"It looks like a big wad of chewing gum," said Tracy. "It doesn't look like a claw."

Tracy was right. Sonny's picture could have been anything. It must not have taken him more than a minute to draw it. It was black.

"He only used one crayon," said Roger.

"It's not fair to get a badge for only using one crayon," said Lisa in disgust.

Mary Beth read her piece about the baby shark named Scamper. Everyone laughed and clapped.

"That was good," said Molly.

When it was Roger's turn, he got up and read, "'There were mummies in the museum, and they were old and they were dead. The end.'"

Rachel waved her hand. "Mrs. Peters, how can he get a badge for one line? That isn't fair!"

"It's not one line," shouted Roger, "it's *two*!"

"It's still too short," said Patty.

Molly had to admit to herself that it was unfair. She had spent hours writing and rewriting and copying her paper over. Then she remembered that she'd had a good time doing it. Apparently Roger hadn't.

Finally it was Molly's turn to read her paper. She wondered if it was too long, or if it was boring, or if everyone would boo her.

But that didn't happen. The title of Molly's paper was "The Pee Wees Almost Go to Jail."

It was a story about a trip to the Center City museum, a stay in a hotel, a mysterious man who looked like a crook, his girlfriend, and her dog, Roger.

And it was about a missing necklace from the museum and how the Pee Wees jumped to the conclusion that Mr. Ross was a crook. It had a surprise ending. Of course it wasn't a surprise to the Pee Wees, because they had been there.

Everyone was spellbound as they listened. They clapped when Molly was done reading.

"But that's not about something in

the museum," Roger piped up.

"Mr. Ross was in the museum!" said Mary Beth, defending her best friend.

"He doesn't live there," said Sonny, "like a mummy or a shark."

"Mummies don't live there," said Kenny. "They're dead."

Mrs. Peters held up her hand.

"Molly has done a very creative project," she said, "on one sheet of paper. She has used her imagination to make the museum trip into a story. It will be a very good record for all of us to keep of our big adventure. It will remind us of the trip, and of the fact that we should not judge people too quickly. I am going to make copies for all of us to put in our scrapbooks."

Most of the Pee Wees applauded again. Some even whistled.

"That was great," said Mary Beth. "I

wish I could make things into stories like that."

"I didn't have to make it into one," said Molly. "That's just what happened."

She was pleased that Mrs. Peters had liked her story. For a change, her wild imagination had not let her down. It had been very useful! It even helped to get her a badge. Rat's knees, writing was fun. And Pee Wee Scouts was fun!

Mrs. Peters passed out the badges. Sonny lost his before the meeting was over. Roger spilled hot chocolate on his.

But Molly felt the badge's soft, silky stitching and admired its bright colors. Then she put it between two pieces of clean paper in her folder. She put the folder safely into her book bag. This was a badge she'd never forget earning. She was sure it would always be her favorite!

We love our country

And our home,

Our school and neighbors too.

As Pee Wee Scouts,

We pledge our best

In everything we do.

Be a Pee Wee Scout!

In *Moans and Groans and Dinosaur Bones,* the Pee Wee Scouts visit a museum.

Have you been to a museum? There are many different kinds. Art museums are full of paintings and sculptures. History museums might focus on anything from arrowheads to airplanes. And science museums usually have displays about space, our planet, and animals—including dinosaurs!

Here are some activities you can try.

1 Draw a Picture

Museums are usually quiet, and that makes them a great place to draw. It's a fun way to make sure you'll always remember your visit. So find a spot to sit

down, make a drawing of your favorite museum item, and write what you've learned about it on the back.

 Be a Cultural Detective

At many museums, you can learn about people who lived long ago. Imagine what it would have been like to be a caveman or a president or an Indian. What would be different about that life? What would be easier than in your life today? What would be harder?

3 Quiz Your Parents

Write down five interesting facts that you learned at the museum. Then try to stump your parents. They'll be amazed at how much you found out in a single afternoon.

4 Build Your Own Museum

As you go through the museum, imagine that *you're* in charge. What displays would be in your perfect museum? Is there anything you absolutely wouldn't have? Why or why not?

5 Don't Forget the Internet

If you can't make it to a museum in person, you can usually visit online. Ask your parents to help you find a famous museum's Web site. Then you can see pictures, learn facts, and maybe even watch movies. It's almost as good as being there!

About the Author

Judy Delton was born and raised in St. Paul, Minnesota. She was the author of more than 200 books for children. She was also successful as a teacher, a speaker, and a class clown. Raising a family  of four children, she used the same mix of humor and seriousness that she considered important parts of any good story. She died in St. Paul in 2001.

About the Illustrator

Alan Tiegreen has illustrated many books for children, including all the Pee Wee Scouts books. He and his wife currently live in Atlanta, Georgia.